Stories from my mother's house

Laura Serrant

To Dick,
I hope you enjoy the
Stories and share ones
of your own – they are
our gift to the world
Laura
March 2023

ISBN: 978-1-7391150-0-5

www.lauraserrant.com

Cover and internal illustrations by Helena Green

DEDICATION

This book is dedicated to my parents Eudora Serrant (nee Toussaint) and John Bonnie Serrant.

They raised myself and my siblings with love, laughter and a strong sense of pride.

Without them there would be no stories, no us and no me.

CONTENTS

Stories from my mother's house

MY MOTHER'S HOUSE

I lived in my mother's house from the age of seven to eighteen. We came to be there after the slum clearance of the 1970s in England. Of course, that's not to say that I hadn't lived somewhere else or have no memory of doing so before that – it's just that this period sits higher in my mind.

My mother and father travelled to England in the late 1950s and early 1960s as part of the Windrush generation. They travelled from Dominica (not the Republic as I learned to say very early on….and still do!). My father travelled first, following one of the continuous calls that came out from the UK to 'rebuild the motherland' that started after the second world war…and to some extent continues today. My mother followed a couple of years later. Imagine, two weeks on a boat – with children in tow! No wonder the Windrush generation were made of stern stuff!

My parents, like many Caribbean families had an extended 'family network'. Brothers, sisters, cousins and a whole range of 'get-me aunties and uncles'; These were 'friends from back home' who were like relatives and because of their 'elder' statuses were always referred to as 'Uncle or

Auntie' by us children as a mark of respect. Woe betide any of us who became too 'bright' and tried to use their first names alone – one look from my mother was enough to dampen any belief that you were 'grown' enough to do so. Even today, in my late 50s, I still use the 'Auntie and Uncle' prefix (just in case). In fact, it was sometimes difficult as a child to work out who was a true blood relation and who was not.

Still is.

In my family I have eight siblings four brothers and four sisters: Three by father (different mother)– who live overseas. Five of us lived in the UK and have the same mother and father. It may seem strange to some of you that I present our family in this way – with no distinction made between full or half siblings as I sometimes hear my non-Caribbean friends talk about. I remember once asking my mother whether Ted was my 'half-brother'…her response? "Half-brother? – which half of him is not your brother?" – she has a point.

We were a noisy, happy family.

Anyway, back to this book. You may ask- why my mother's house?

Home is a very powerful symbol for me. For our family.

My mother's house was a place of belonging and safety. It reflects for me the importance of home and belonging. A place, my place where I go to feel truly me. A place through which I can map my own passage through stages of life.

In this book I recall and recount glimpses of that life and in doing so share with you some of the things which symbolise the importance of home.

The poems in this book reflect what unites us as a family. They may be similar or vastly different to your own experiences but whether they trigger memories that mirror or contrast with your own, they are, our stories of ourselves. They map out our journeys so far, what has bought us to this place in our lives......and so house our very essence, our power to be truly human.

ROOMS WITH A VIEW

This book is organised into rooms. Each room introduces a different aspect of memory, of experience and of reflection. They begin with my own picture of that room in my mother's house and then link to the 'stories of being' in that space and what it means to me, to us.

Each room in my mother's house had a purpose. They all did something. As children, we all knew what was allowed, or not allowed, in each room.

Despite this, each room had the capacity to surprise us. to catch us out. .....Leading to a wonderful shower of memories of good times or cringing recollections of being told off for breaking a sacred rule.

Each of the rooms I share here is described from my memory of that time. I am now 58 years old so not surprisingly, some of these events have become a little altered in my mind and in my memory. They may also have been influenced by many years of retelling these stories between myself and my brothers and sisters. Their memories and their versions of the truth have become inextricably combined with my own. Evenings weekends and afternoons of laughter and recall have moulded and shaped the stories I share here.

So, read with an open mind but also with the knowledge that what I describe and share with you here is not from a single event or from one year. They are rather a combination of the strongest memories and the deepest feelings I had between the ages of 7 to 18 when I lived in my mother's house.

For those of you who like numbers and the historians among you, these stories span the years 1970 to 1982.

My pictures of home, my mother's house, may not be the same as yours. But as you journey with me through the rooms of my mother's house, I hope you will see that each room holds within it some of our shared thoughts, feelings and experiences as people.

I share my stories from My Mother's House with you as poems and reflections- opportunities to travel with me, glimpse my world and remember journeys of your own.

THESE are the stories worth telling.

Our untold stories of self.

2 THE KITCHEN

"The kitchen table, a simmering pot and my mother – the heartspace where soul food is prepared – nourishing mind, body and spirit".

THE KITCHEN: STORIES OF BELONGING

The kitchen in my mother's house was the first room.

As a child it was the only entry and exit to the house that was fully available to you. There was no way that before the age of 16 you could freely enter or exit the house using the front door, unless of course you were accompanied by an adult - Entry via the front door was definitely for 'big people'

The kitchen was the family and friends' entrance.

The way into the centre of the house and my mother's domain.

In the kitchen there was a central table. The fitted units hugged the walls on three sides. The kitchen units were a very fashionable burnt orange colour, very 1970s. They were my mother's pride and joy. She had chosen the colour; she had chosen the layout and in here she was definitely Queen. The cupboards always overflowed with food. I don't remember walking into that room from the outside without seeing or smelling evidence of food being prepared, shared or cooked. One wall of the kitchen was almost fully taken up by a large window above the sink which looked out over the very big garden – as a large family, we were fortunate to be rehoused to one of the bigger council houses on the estate. From the kitchen window you could see the grassed area where we played, and beyond that, the huge vegetable patches and greenhouse where my dad grew enough vegetables to feed us, and a few other families throughout the year. The garden was definitely my Dad's domain.

The windowsill in the kitchen was crowded with plants – my mother had a way with plants. They were throughout the house, but on the kitchen windowsills they seemed to thrive, as if buoyed into looking their best by the vision of their compatriots outside. The cooker which was gas and housed to the right as you entered was usually on. If something wasn't being fried, boiled or simmered on the top of the stove, then it was being baked in the oven.

My mother's family in Dominica baked bread. This family industry continued when she came to England.

Every week during my childhood we had fresh baked bread, in fact I remember it being a treat for us to have mothers' pride white bread bought from the shop. I didn't appreciate the wonderful value of home baked bread as a child, particularly as I wanted to have the soft shop bought variety as my friends did in their lunch boxes.

Initially when we were younger my mother baked all the bread. Every week, on a Saturday, she baked enough bread to feed seven people for a full week. I remember the very large pink - yes pink! - mixing bowl that she used to mix and knead what seemed to me, as a small child, a huge mountain of dough. In fact, I remember at about the age of 8 when my mother used to allow me to stand on a chair and knead the dough for a while - the sides of the bowl were so deep that I remember it digging into my armpits as I stretched on to my tip toes to reach down to the bottom of the bowl as instructed by my mother so as 'not to waste' any of the mixture. As I grew older (and got taller) I was trusted to both prepare and mix the weekly bread dough. This progressed to me taking over the bread making, together with my sister and baking the bread supply for the whole family. I was only released from this duty at the age of 18 when I left home. Our duties began with buying the fresh yeast from a shop called Burton's in the town centre and measuring out then completing all the preparations of soaking the yeast, adding the ingredients and overseeing the transformation from dough to batches of Cobs (Nottinghamshire word for what you may call bread buns, baps, rolls or barm cakes; depending on where you are from).

I am ashamed to say but I have never baked bread since.

Bread making aside, the kitchen in my mother's house was a place of stories, of talking and learning.

Around that table life happened.

As children and all the way through to my teenage years, we did our homework at that table. When we were younger it was a way for my mother to monitor our work, to listen to us read and to make sure that we didn't waste the valuable education that we had been gifted. You see my mother left school relatively early. As the eldest daughter in a large family, whose father died before she reached her teenage years, she had to leave school in order to help raise her younger siblings and to help her mother in the family shop. My father had a similar time span at school and so, like many other Caribbean parents they valued education and the opportunity to attend school as the most important gift they could give us. At that table therefore, we as children slowly fulfilled the vision our parents had for us to learn, to understand and to be educated.

Our education and learning in that kitchen and at that table went beyond what was written in our schoolbooks.

Through the kitchen on any given day, passed a wonderful kaleidoscope of family, friends and visitors. By listening and watching our elders in that kitchen, we heard tales of their past, stories and chatter recounting and recalling episodes from life now and plans for lives in the future. 'Busy chatter' - that is the phrase which best describes the atmosphere in the kitchen when anyone 'passed by'.

In that kitchen the radio was always on.

Music, discussions and news came and went. My mother kept a grip on what was happening in the world through her radio – right down to the latest tunes and political viewpoints…and she had an opinion on all of it.

One of my most vivid memories of my mother, in that kitchen, is her multitasking like no one I ever knew - this picture is one of her at her best: Simultaneously baking, cooking and preparing a meal while she talks with, about and of, our family with the latest visitor. And all the time being able to watch what we were doing as children, feed us AND the visitor, stopping occasionally to detail a really important part of the story she was telling or to sing and dance along to a tune on the radio which reminded her of days past. All of this done without missing a beat - that was my mother the very epitome of a one woman show!

That table and that kitchen is, for me, the soul of my mother's house. It is the place where we came to understand our family's past and ourselves.

Our place of belonging: Where bellies, minds and hearts were fed to overflowing and where anyone who took a place there was welcomed as part of the family.

As a child it was a place of magic and wonder.
A place where I felt fully safe,
fully accepted
and fully myself.

Welcome to Our House

Welcome to our house.

It is not perfect

It does not make our hearts sing

and our smiles breakout

because it is perfect.

and we, are certainly not perfect.

We do not welcome you

because of what makes you the same as others.

We do not welcome you

because you make us feel our difference.

We welcome you

because we feel the joy of being loved by

and being with you.

We welcome you because

we are certainly not the same

as others you may have known.

Welcome to our house

we do not demand, nor expect

perfection from you.

We love and cherish you

for who you are,

and for the fearful imperfections

that are part of you.

We welcome you because

you are different and

you make us feel differently,

so differently,

from others who came before.

Welcome to our house.

We welcome you

because of *your* difference.

As different and

as imperfect as we are.

Here you are always welcome.

Come in

and sit.

And continue to be

your imperfectly, perfect self

Welcome to our house.

Family Ties

Family ties.

The bonds that bind

us together.

What centres our family,

are the soul-filled spaces where we meet.

The very things that make us special,

uniquely us.

The ease with which we connect

and our souls entwine.

Over the years.

Over the stories.

Over the arguments

and the laughter.

Despite the divisions of time and space

is the surety that comes

with each conversation,

each reimagining,

and each retelling of

THAT day.

These are the things that reflect

and illustrate,

the depth of the connections we feel.

The bonds that nourish our souls.

Linking us to our past

and fulfilling the needs of the next generation.

Family ties.

The place where we come to understand the past

and ourselves.

A Child's Eyes

With my child's eyes
in the mornings
I bask in the brilliance of her smile.
I see her in my mind's eye
and in that moment,
I look into her eyes
and see me reflected.
In those precious spaces,
between sleep and awakening,
I feel her.
The warm welcoming smile that says
"Good morning, morning my child,
I'm happy to see you"
I catch my breath
at the smooth contours of her face
turned to me,
and searching mine

With smiles of love

Checking for signs of health,

for signs of peace.

As years pass, I see more of myself

residing within me, as her

and her as me.

That smile has always reflected

her commitment to me.

My mind and my heart swell.

Each inch of her lovely self

I imagine holding me close and sustaining

my need to be with her:

To keep her with me as a point of Remembrance,

long after her physical place has gone.

This is my place of precious refuge

until tomorrow's dawn.

My Mother's Kitchen.

I am from my mother's kitchen.

I am from freshly baked bread macaroni cheese.

I am from plants on the windowsill: 'busy lizzies', homegrown thyme and 'mother of thousands'.

I am from laughter and giggling, plaiting hair and doing homework.

I am from seven siblings three girls and four boys.

I am from the sounds of the radio, dancing and singing at the top of our voices.

I am from "you are good enough…just as you are".

I am from "be the best you can be".

I am from Sunday Mass and reading in church.

I am from cricket trips, dominoes and a brandy for Dad.

I am from Dasheen, Yam, Souse and Johnny cakes.

I am from remembering when there wasn't enough, but my mother made it 'stretch'.

I am from putting the pot on the stove, when the doorbell rings.

I am from nothing shop bought and everything homemade or grown in the garden.

I am from early mornings watching my dad go out to work before light.

I am from late nights with mum going out to work when dad came in.

I am from sitting, listening to the 'aunties' put the world to rights.

I am from waiting to be excused from the table.

I am from cups of tea and always time for a chat.

I am from "come in, sit down" and "of course there's enough to go round".

I am from my mother's kitchen

You, Us, We

Because of you, I have found myself.

In us, there is a strength that allows me to stand tall, proud of who I am

And what I,

we,

will become.

Through you, my spirit is lifted

to dream, to hope, to dare.

Yet rooted firmly in knowledge of Us,

allowing me to Stand tall,

make mistakes

and move forward again.

With you, I have no doubts,

We will thrive and shine

As we were always destined to do.

As part of you,

worries about worth, truth or belonging are calmed.

We have gifted me

Love,

Care,

And pride.

Through you, and because of us

I am at peace

I am seen

I am me.

Soul food

Eat.

Feed your soul and sustain yourself.

We must remember to feed the soul

We must remember to laugh, to eat the fruits

That allow the feelings of joy, however fleeting,

To embalm our souls with their juices and their light.

"Have some more…there's plenty".

Food can always 'stretch'.

Make room for another – set a place.

Take more feel the fullness rise in your soul

Feel the simple pleasures of being together

Remember to laugh, to listen and to hear the sound of ourselves

"Ease up yourself"

Allow ourselves to just be.

Drink.

We must remember to love

That priceless gift of time.

Remember to value each other and ourselves

One without the other, leads to famine.

Eat your fill.

Let your soul shine

Embracing the wonderful joy of life.

Of this life.

3 THE LIVING ROOM

The place where imaginations are fuelled and minds are set free

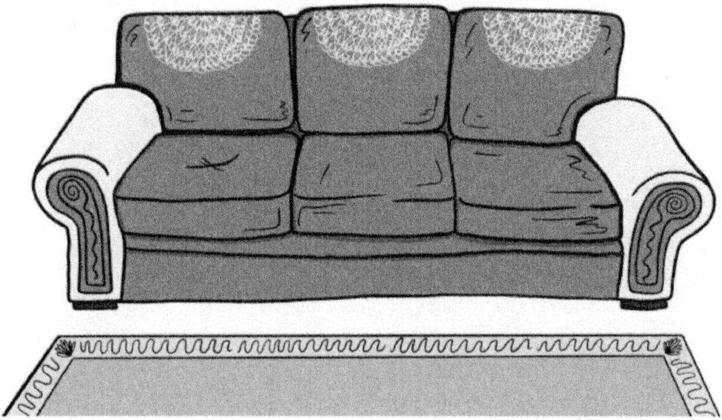

THE LIVING ROOM: STORIES OF LEARNING AND TOGETHERNESS

The living room in my mother's house was a happy place. A chameleon of a room that served a myriad of purposes.

Entering via the frosted glass door directly from the kitchen, you were faced with a long room stretching out to your right into the extension which overlooked the garden and housed the dining room table.

Directly in front of you was a large 3-seater settee. When we first moved into my mother's house, it was an imitation leather settee. Well, the back, arms and frame of the settee were a pale brown coloured 'leather' - but the seating cushions were brown fabric.

This settee, or sofa as you may have called it in your home, had travelled with us from the previous house. I am not exactly sure when my parents purchased this item. It seems to have always been there. It appears in many photographs which predate our movement into my mother's house. In fact, this particular settee features in the black and white christening pictures of my youngest sister; taken in the front room of our previous house in 1969 (and it doesn't look particularly new then!). Later, my parents 'up graded' to another 3 seater – still brown, but now one of the more of a chocolate and pale sand coloured fabric variety. In both cases, the settee had the same function and purpose in my mother's house.

My father took his rests on that settee.

You see when I lived in my mother's house, my dad rose at 3 or 4 o'clock every morning in the week - leaving before daylight to make sure he got to work by 5:30am. He worked in the heavy steel industry – making the moulds for the items forged in the castings furnace of a local boiler works. A far cry from his work with the farmworkers in the open air of our beloved Dominica. He worked 8 hours or more in the foundry in the searing heat of the furnace, taking salt tablets every four or so hours to counteract the water loss from sweating. When he returned home and had eaten, he often dozed off.... lying on the settee: One hand behind his head, and his eyes closed. However, somehow he was always able to hear if we children were getting out of hand or had the audacity to turn the TV over (when we thought he was asleep) before the programme he was watching - usually the news - had finished.

Anyway, I digress, the large settee sat centre stage in the living room - flanked on the on its right by the sliding doors to the Front room; and on its left by a large arm chair.

My mother's armchair.

Actually, truth be told, this armchair was initially my *parents* armchair. Both my mother and father used it.

My father took his weekday meals there. He was served his dinner on a tray during the week when he returned from work. It was our job as children, once we were old enough, to carry to him, 'his' tray laden with the food and a glass of water, prepared by my mother.

In later years, after my mother retired and when she became less a little less mobile, this armchair was raised on blocks by social services to save her sore hip and to help her get up from the chair with a little more ease.

But that was much later.

As a child, the living room was a place where we came together. Adults and children had equal space and place in this room. The room also housed the television, an array of plants, a small child's stool with a green/white woven plastic seat and the small nest of tables. This nest of tables could be pulled out and placed at the feet of the latest visitor - so they had somewhere to rest the refreshments that were always on hand. Alternatively, they acted as a makeshift dining table for one of the many small children (nieces, nephews, cousins and friends) that frequented my mother's house.

Behind the frosted door there was space for one chair. One dining chair.

This chair rarely moved from that spot. In fact, its only regular outing was to travel to the other end of the living room where the dining table sat. And this only happened at Christmas, Easter or when there was a large family meal that required more than the six chairs that were placed around the table.

More often than not the chair behind the door was the visitor's chair. On occasions when the adults' conversation was friendly, informal and not covering any subjects unsuitable for children, the visitors sat here and spoke with my mother or father who were sitting in the parents' chair. In my mind's eye I can still see the succession of my father and mother's friends who popped in for an informal chat while 'passing by': Perched on the chair, recounting the latest joke or message from 'home'.

The television sat halfway between the seating and the dining area facing the settee. It was a large television, the old box type with its imitation teak casing and large buttons.

A beast of an item on black metal legs.

I remember my father being very proud of this television which had a remote control. However, this did not prevent him from asking one of us children to turn the TV over as we were usually seated on the floor, closest to it.

The living room was a place of learning. Our lessons took many forms. From the formal homework set by school which was done at the dining room table when we had graduated to secondary school. As previously mentioned, primary school homework was completed in the kitchen under the watch full eye of my mother. Seated opposite each other, my sister and I poured over books about history, biology and tried to understand the complexities of quadratic equations. Occasionally stopping to look outside at my younger sister playing on the grass or my mother hanging out the washing on the line that crossed the lawn.

Less formal learning, but somehow even more important, happened in the living room. This was where we began to learn about the world outside my mother's house.

The television bought some knowledge of experiences different to our own. Other experiences and learning came from the overheard snippets of conversation between my mother and my father, or the visitors. My parents both spoke patois - something my mother sometimes politely described to English speaking visitors as 'broken

French'. In essence it was the mother tongue, the spoken language of Dominica. In the living room we learned how to hear, listen and speak the language. So, our learning covered what was happening in Dominica, the Caribbean and our homeland family as much as what was occurring in Nottingham or in the UK at that time.

Lessons about life – good and bad - were learned in the living room. I was there when I heard about my first niece being born, where I shared secrets with my cousins, first saw my mother cry and where I learned my paternal grandmother had died.

The living room also contained books. They were often stacked beneath the sideboard that ran along one wall in the extension next to the dining table.

Reading was a key part of our learning.

My parents, who for differing reasons had left school before the age of 15, were almost fanatically committed to making sure that their children benefited from all the education on offer. If we didn't have homework set by the school, we had reading allocated to us by my father. Despite the living room also housing the television, reading was the priority. At reading or homework time, the television remained switched off. A silent black box in the centre of the room.

Learning about culture and place extended beyond language and stories from 'home'. In the living room we learned about our position as children relative to adults. For example, in our large family, small children always sat on the floor when we gathered together. Adults took priority on the settee and any higher seating. When we grew and got older, our seating position changed. As teenagers we also sat on the settee, unless of course we had adult visitors. In that case we got up silently, without being asked and moved to the dining area. Leaving the comfortable chairs for the adults to sit. Woe betides you if you didn't get up before being asked to do so by my mother.

Good manners and biding your elders were an unspoken rule.

Of course, when adults were missing, the living room became a place of excitement and learning different lessons. It became a place where our imaginations we're allowed to run riot. Some of the best times in the living room were when the adults retired to the front room (more of the front room later). In those times children ruled the living room space.

We could make dens under the table; we could run from one end of the room to the other; chasing, laughing and giggling… with siblings, with cousins and with friends. We could play games such as dobby-off-ground; where we tried to travel from one end of the room to the other without touching the floor or being caught by the person who was 'on'. 'Dobby' is a Nottingham word. You may have called it tig, tag or something similar. We played cards at the table, we discussed our latest adventures, our dreams and we planned what we would do if we were rich.

The living room in my mother's house was a place where we were together as a family, as siblings and as individuals in a large, loud, social network.

Here we transitioned from children to adults.

It was where we first learned about life, about the world, about family and about responsibility.

Strange speech

What is strange about discussions across generations

are the very things make it special.

The ease with which we connect

and our words entwine

despite the divisions of time and space.

The surety that comes from speaking

in languages

old and ancient

written and unwritten.

The ability of young ears

to hear and understand

words so different

from those they hear every day.

The grace with which the elders move

effortlessly from one to the other

reflecting and illustrating

the depth of their connections

with the past

our present

and our futures.

The homeland

in this land.

Speaking, repeating,

sharing and connecting us:

One generation to another.

One time space to another.

No longer strange,

but comforting.

Uniting us

in learning

about us.

History lessons

Histories.

His and her stories.

Sitting and listening,

to shadows of laughter,

of pain and of past.

Histories.

Outlining the times

when calm and safety

were part of their dreams and desires.

Recounting times

of upset of unrest

and a finding joy in every day actions.

Histories.

No Blacks.

No dogs.

No Irish.

But despite this

learning to laugh

learning to find the fun.

In this strange land

Where we landed.

Histories.

The context in which we find ourselves,

celebrate ourselves,

and

lost something of ourselves

and ached for a sense of belonging.

Histories.

For what we have found.

What we have learned.

And what we can yet achieve.

His-story, and her-story.

The chink of the glass.

The warmth of the food

and the closeness of the friendships.

The pathways to learning

that above all

to ourselves we must be true.

His-story, and her-story.

The blessings that bind us

That teach us to grow strong:

With the roots that keep us steady

and the wings that allow us to dream.

His-story and her-story.

Past.

Present.

And hope for the future.

His-story and her-story.

The beginning of their story,

and our story.

Promises kept

I promise

to remember your face.

In the mornings, rising early

hearing the sounds

of your preparation.

Quiet steps

the occasional cough.

I promise

to watch your face as you sleep.

To see you press your hands

against your forehead,

the wrinkles rising and falling

through your silent dreams.

I smell your scent as you pass.

Clean, fresh,

with a little splash

of something …wonderful.

I promise

to etch your face in my mind.

So it may soothe my soul

in the quiet times.

I watch you press your face to a small child.

Making them laugh,

with your deep slow voice.

I promise

to leave the imprint of you on my heart.

So I may hold it

in safe keeping

until you return.

I promise

to take the time to show the world.

With each breath that I take.

how much you've influenced

my thinking

and my thoughts.

How much you mean to me.

I promise

to treasure each moment,

I had with you.

Each one you blessed me with.

I promise.

I promise.

Today

Today,

we danced!

Today,

we laughed! We joked!

and re imagined.

Today

we listened to the sounds of our hearts.

To love, to laughter, to care

and to hope.

Today

we imagined

the bright skies

and the dancing stars

of worlds yet to be seen.

Today

we built a fort.

We built an island

where we could dance and jump

and splash, next to the seashore.

Today

we sat in fairy castles

and sang songs

from our made-up dreams!

Today

we laughed *so* hard

our sides hurt!

Today

we whispered, and smiled

and slept.

Today

We played.

Hair

Sitting on the floor.

Between her knees.

Crossed legged.

And staring at the TV.

The smell of shampoo

And freshly washed bodies

Mixes with the remains of the polish

From this morning's cleaning.

Slow humming

With the occasional break out into a hymn.

As hair is parted and 'grease' applied

From the back of her hand

To my scalp.

My head rests against her knees

As I absorb the sounds

and moving pictures in front of me.

The involuntary wince and shrug of my shoulders

As the wide comb

Fights with a proud curl

That refuses to give way.

Feeling the quick movement of her fingers

Twisting and smoothing

Rapidly and rhythmically

Teasing sections into plaits and coils

Which now lie flat to my head.

A final seal of oil across my forehead

And I am done.

Time for bed.

View from a window

Inside

Watching the wind

As it catches the washing

Each time she lifts it

from the pink plastic basket.

She balances 4 pegs

Two in hand, two in mouth.

Strong hands hold a sheet steady against the line.

While a few quick movements

From hand to sheet

Then mouth to hand

Has it secured.

A glance back into the window

Seeing us at our homework.

A quick nod, and wave to ask

'you okay?'

She walks to the end of the path

And calls to my dad.

In the garden, digging and planting

As usual.

He stops, and nods his head

In acknowledgement of her call.

I watch

As they speak soundlessly

Arms waving, heads nodding

And teeth smiling.

My eyes dart between them.

Admiring the noiseless chatter

Of their conversation.

She turns and walks back

Towards the house.

To us.

Head down and I focus again

On the work set.

The knock on the window catches me.

I see her standing

Hands on hips,

her headscarf blowing in the breeze.

she mouths the word

And indicates "tea"

then turns back to her task.

As I rise

and move away from the window,

I see her standing

And surveying the washing line.

Then with a slow sigh, and an exhale,

she bends to retrieve another garment.

Ready to start again.

4 THE FRONT ROOM

"A sacred space – The centre of our respectability: a space of legacy, remembering and belonging.

THE FRONT ROOM: STORIES OF IDENTITY AND CELEBRATION

The front room was a place for adults.

Nestled between the living room and the hallway, it was to some extent the physical centre of the house. It was my parents' pride and joy. A crowded, colourful space which housed all their most treasured possessions: Pictures, ornaments and pieces of furniture which documented our family - past and present – and in doing so, recorded how far they….. we, had come.

In the front room our heritage, family memories and traditions were displayed. Faded pictures of my parents on their wedding day, relatives who had died long before we were born – 'the ancestors' and those who lived far away in the Caribbean. The large, framed map of Dominica took pride of place – where we were taught at an early age to point out *exactly* where we were from. Our very identities as proud Dominicans living in Britain were reflected here.

The chimney breast in the room was graced by a large wooden fire surround, which framed the 'three sectioned' gas fire. The polished teak shone – fresh from the regular weekly polishing it had received over decades. Always smelling of 'mister sheen' but still needing to be refreshed every Saturday morning; firstly, by our mother, and then by us kids, when we grew old enough to be trusted not to break any of the many ornaments that adorned it.

Ornaments of various sizes, shapes and materials were crammed into every part of this fireplace. And indeed, all corners of the front room. Hanging from the walls, framed in pictures or sitting in pride of place on every available surface – they sat proudly…slowly collecting dust within the week and then returned to their sparkling best after the weekend clean. Every surface on which they sat was also protected – by a network of crocheted and lace doilies.

During my childhood the room appeared to change – yet at the same time strangely remain the same. The ornaments were added to as we grew – expanded by gifts and souvenirs given to my parents, well my mother mainly, either by us as children or visitors to our home. They were a living library – documenting our travels on school trips: clogs from Holland, snow globes from Paris and even small plastic 'Virgin Mary' shaped bottles of holy water from Lourdes. All had their place in the front room.

The sofa in the front room was a magnificent feat of engineering – 1970s style! A huge corner suite in dark patterned 'velour'. It took up three quarters of the space in the room, sitting under the window opposite the fireplace. The curved sections of the sofa were teak, like the fireplace and provided convenient 'side' tables on which visitors could rest their drink or snack next to them (on the obligatory doily or placemat of course). This had to be achieved with a level of skill, so as to carefully avoid knocking over the purposefully placed ceramic fruit or glass vase of plastic flowers, whose usual place it was.

In front of the corner suite – between it and the fireplace – was a round glass topped coffee table with a teak frame (the 1970s and my mother were great fans of teak). The centre of the table had the best crocheted doily, with stiff frilled edges which defied gravity and stood to attention around an equally impressive centre piece; at one time a white swan with artificial flowers in its 'back' between its semi-raised wings, another time, a large vase of flowers, plastic gladioli – my mother's favourite. In both cases, these grand items were ritually washed in the sink with soapy water (yes, even the flowers) as part of the weekend cleaning regime.

On the floor in front of the fireplace was an imitation "sheepskin rug'. Despite the front room being fully carpeted, the rug remained. I remember as a child lying on that rug, during the few times when we were allowed in the front room on a Sunday afternoon. I watched the orange-coloured flames in the sections of the gas fire flicker, as the light faded. My mother, seated on the sofa, hummed to herself, or silently turned the pages of her bible, quietly mouthing the words of scripture as she read.

The front room was a symbol of our respectability. The place where formal visitors and priests were shown. Where my parents went to talk about things children should not hear. Where dad did the pools and read the Sunday paper and where mum read her prayer book and sent thoughts up for family members, both dead and alive, after church.

One of the things that struck me most about the front room in my mother's house, was how similar it was to the front rooms of my cousins, other family members and indeed most of the Caribbean friends we had. There were elements of our front room in all theirs too – The overcrowded mantlepieces, groaning under the strain of its 'bounty' of ornaments; the radiogram sitting in the corner of the room, which housed the turntable on which my dad played records; the ornate glass cabinet with sliding glass doors and glass shelves bursting with all the best china and glassware that were cleaned and washed religiously, but never really drank from; the 3 ducks of varying graduated sizes hanging over the fireplace, lined up as if in flight; the pineapple or peach plastic ice bucket which was used on high days, parties and holidays to dispense ice to guests to cool their drinks; and of course, the hologrammed religious pictures that followed your gaze around the room and reminded you of the high expectations for your behaviour through the words from the bible.

As a small child I once asked my father why all the Caribbean families we knew or visited seemed to have these particular items in their house – he answered "when you arrive on the boat, they line you all up and give you one of 'each' to get you started".....I was 18 years old before I realised this was not exactly true!

However, the front room in my mother's house did hold a shared identity with most west Indian front rooms: it was a place which signified our position as a family. It was a living record of my parents' work and tenacity, coming to England and establishing themselves despite the challenges they faced.

Despite the racism.

The front room signified our belonging, family and respectability. It signified us.

Long before my parents and other migrants like them were accepted in clubs and other social spaces in their neighbourhoods, their homes, and the front room in particular was a place for coming together, for socialising with friends and family…a place of entertainment 'Caribbean style'. A place for parties.

My mum and dad knew how to throw a party (or a fete)! In preparations for a party my parents were in their element. Each had a role before, during and after – they were like a well-oiled machine– each knew what was expected of them and executed their duties with precision.

Weeks before the actual date, my mother would go

into planning mode. Each week a little extra food and a bottle of something 'strong' to lace the punch she would make on the day, would be added to the regular family shopping basket. All items would be carefully 'laid away' for the party, either at the back of the wardrobe in mum and dad's bedroom, or in the deep freeze in the living room. It was one of the few times my dad would 'shop' on his own and without instruction: Making sure there was an extra brandy, whisky, or rum to top up my mum's purchases.

A few days before the big day my mother moved into another gear; meat would be defrosted, seasoned and the cooking would start. This scene was being simultaneously replicated by similar activities at the houses of my 'aunties' - both of the blood relations and 'get me' variety previously spoken about. These women were some of my mother's closest friends, who, like my mother herself, would have died before they came to a fete with 'their two hands swinging' (empty handed).

The morning of the party would see the front room as a focal point, a hive of activity. All the ornaments had to be polished, of course. Freshly laundered doilies and crocheted seat backs were ironed (again) and in place. We children were given a myriad of jobs running to and from the kitchen or other parts of the house under instruction from my mother to fetch this, carry that and go and check on the other – our legs moving as fast as we could and arms constantly laden with the items from the latest errand. All the time trying not to spill, disturb or mess up anything that was 'for the party'.

My dad would sort the music and entertainment for the evening. He would carefully sit down on the floor in the front room and line up his vinyl records, from Mighty Sparrow, Explainer, Arrow, Carleen Davies, Cynthia Schloss to Byron Lee, and the Dragonnaires.... and the list goes on. All the while listening to the soothing voices of Jim Reeves, Skeeter Davis and Bobby Bare; not forgetting Pat Boone. A strange combination indeed – sorting soca and calypso, listening to country music! By the end of the morning, he had his playlist - Soca, reggae, calypso, 'rock steady' and little 'whining' music for the early hours.

In truth, the party preparations took place all through the house; the kitchen, living room, and bathrooms but it was orchestrated from the front room.

As a child, I loved when my parents had a party. Under strict instructions not to get in the way of 'big people', we watched from the stairs as the guests arrived. Aunts, female older cousins, wives and girlfriends passed us in a colourful parade like exotic bids: fabulous clothes, heels clicking on the plastic runner from the front door, lipstick shining, and hair coiffured to a 'T' – Results of either their own skills or a full day spent at the hairdressers. Each also bearing their offering for the feast. The men followed sporting freshly laundered open necked shirts, teamed with crisply pressed trousers with a crease sharp enough to cut bread, and smelling of cologne. Some of the more 'stoosh' among them having a matching handkerchief in the top pocket of their blazers.

The arrivals chattered and greeted each other loudly; laughing and joking, stopping occasionally to acknowledge us children as they passed. Pinching our cheeks and telling us how much we had grown. Those who came with their own children, our cousins and friends, would linger a moment at the stairs as they deposited their children with us; giving them the same warning our mother had given us earlier 'not to show me up' and to 'stay out of big people's way'.

As the house filled, the music started. My dad's carefully selected records were played, and everyone danced. The later it got, more people danced. Shoulders swaying, hips shaking, laughing, and singing at the top of their voices to the sounds of Mighty Sparrow, Explainer and the rest of the crew! There was no air-conditioning in my mother's house, after all, it was the Midlands, and we were in 1970/80s England. As the room got hotter due to the growing crowd and the dancing, windows were opened. The adults sweated, women fanned themselves, and their partners with their rainbow-coloured fans, dancing harder and closer together as the tempo of the music increased. We children played at parties. Daring to run through the house during hide and seek or darting across the front room through the sea of legs and scent. In those relatively small spaces of the house party, the hearts and minds of children and adults alike, were free.

Throughout the evening food was served. The cold buffet laid out earlier on the table in the living room and the carefully placed bowls of peanuts, crisps and nibbles were buoyed up by 'hard food'. Days in the making and designed to soak up the alcohol we feasted on curry goat, souse, black pudding, fried chicken, rice and peas, homemade coleslaw, beef patties, 'johnny cakes' and hard-dough bread. My mother and the aunties expertly carried food on trays, weaving in and out of the dancers to make sure all were fed. Never spilling a drop on their best clothes and lipstick firmly in place. Later as we became older, this was a task given to us children. A sign that we were responsible, but also that we were becoming adults, legitimately allowed to be a little part of 'big people tings'.

No-one left my mother's house hungry. It was the rule. Parties were even more important. Stomachs, souls and minds were filled here. Equally my parents would not allow anyone to leave who was too drunk. Anyone they believed was too bad to go home safely was persuaded to 'sleep where you fall' – often found by us children the next morning under a table, in the bath or somewhere in the front room.

As the night progressed the music changed from the frantic beats of Soca to the rhythmic sounds of 'Rocksteady'. The party continued into the early morning – but long before this, we children had fallen asleep, often lying end to end on the beds with our cousins who had arrived with their parents - lulled into our dreams by the sounds of the beat and adult chatter coming up from the front room below into our ears. Sounds which encased all that precious about who we were, what we had been and could be as a family.

The sounds of home.

A brief comment…

As a nurse, I could not help but begin this chapter, with this first poem.

It's a story not of my mother's house per se but the journey that my parents took like many others to travel, establish themselves and achieve so much in a 'strange' land. Written in 2018 to mark 70 years of the NHS and the arrival of the Empire Windrush at Tilbury docks, London. In 2022 it was selected as the inscription to stand alongside the National Windrush Monument at Waterloo station in London, England. It is dedicated to my parents and The Windrush Generation who shaped 'This England'. Documenting in a different way, all that makes us who we are – just as the living library that was my mother's front room.

You called….and we came

You called…and we came.

In ships bigger than anything we had seen,

dwarfing our islands and covering them

in the shadows of smoke and noise.

Crowded, excited voices filled the air,

traveling to the 'motherland'

- over weeks, over oceans that threatened to engulf us.

Driven by a wish, a call to save, to rebuild

and support efforts to establish 'health for all'

in the aftermath of war.

You called….and we came.

Women and men of position in our homelands;

nurses with a pride in the excellence of our care.

With experience of management, organisation

and a sense of duty.

We appeared.

Smiling and eager to work on the wards and clinics

of this England.

You called….and we came.

Our big hearts, skilful hands and quick minds

encased in our skins - of a darker hue.

Which had shimmered and glowed

in our sunnier climes..

But now signified our difference

- our un-belonging.

Matrons became assistants

Nurses became like chambermaids.

All the while striving to fulfil our promise

- to succour, to serve, to care.

You called….and we came.

The blue of the sister's uniform

- seemed as far away from us as the moon.

Unreachable by our dark hands in this cold land.

But we were made of sterner stuff.

The hot sun, which once beat down on our ancestors,

when they too left their lands,

Shone within us.

Forging our hearts and minds

with the resistance of Ebony.

You called….and we came.

Rising like the Phoenix,

from the heat of rejection.

We cared, we worked, and we organised.

Until the quickness of our brains

and the excellence of our care

made it hard for you to contain us.

And slowly, so slowly,

the blue uniforms had dark and lighter bodies beneath them.

The professional care in our touch

was valued despite the strangeness of our speech

and the kinks in our hair.

You called….and we came.

A new millennium - new hopes spread across this land.

New populations, engaging and reflecting

the varied, diverse and vibrant nature of these shores.

Challenging and reflecting on leadership for health.

Moves to melt the 'snow' at the peaks of our profession.

Recognising the richness of our kaleidoscope nation.

Where compassion, courage and diversity are reflected

In our presence and our contribution:

Not only the hopes and dreams of our ancestors.

- Human values needed to truly lead change…and add value.

Remember… you called.

Remember… you called.

YOU. Called.

Remember, it was us, who came.

Watching Adults Dance

Red, Gold, Green and Blue.

Flashes of colour moving in time

To the beat and rhythm of the music.

Eyes half closed.

Lips soundlessly mouthing the words

and bodies swaying as if carried by the sounds.

An intricate web of movements, telling stories of

Past lives, homelands and belonging.

Adorning the room like bright exotic birds.

Outfits pressed and cleaned just for this occasion.

Hair coiffured, and worn as crowns

- speaking of our royalty.

Bodies twirling, revealing stories of joy, freedom,
youth and remembrance.

Quick movements and subtle changes of pace

Which my child's eyes race to absorb.

The air heavy with scent.

Fragrances filling my nostrils

with senses of the stories, the emotions, and love.

Mesmerising me with their performance

While the African beats pound in my chest.

Watching my histories come alive and be presented before me in a glorious display.

Watching adults' dance.

A Room with a View

Ourselves past, present and future.

Recordings of how far we have come,

And the potential of our future selves.

Strangely familiar, yet unmet faces of the ancestors

Keep watch over us from their golden frames.

Seemingly nodding approvement or disapproval

At the actions of our generations.

An array of ornaments documents our journeys so far

And map out our achievements and aspirations

- as clearly as the three flightless ducks

That signpost our unstoppable movement upwards.

The glass cabinet

Seems to sigh under the weight of its precious cargo.

Displaying our treasured collections

Depicting movement of social positions

from 'essential for survival' to 'for best and

respectful'.

The familiar soothing sound of ticking from the carriage wall clock

Steady and true, marking out the passage of days, weeks and years.

Chiming out a dependable cry on the hour, and half hour late into the night.

All items in their place, and have their place

A view of our family, in time and space.

Ode to the ancestors

In the depth of knowing your presence

We feel the promise of hope and care.

In the warmth of your eyes

Watching us through faded pictures

We see the focus of your strength

And know that if lost, you will find us again.

In the sense of your touch, silent yet purposeful

We are transferred to a place

Where our spirit is soothed,

yet burns with an inner force, as if on fire.

In the calm of your words, handed down through generations

We are held on solid ground and our breathing

becomes rhythmic and steady once more.

The power from you, the belief in you,

forged through pain, joy and determination

Has brought us to a place of belonging.

Trusting once more in ourselves, our legacy and our destiny.

Through you and because of you, we are, and will be

Forever one;

From one come many

And many are one.

One family, one people.

Nature Isle

Island of Nature.

You sustain us

And fill us with pride.

Land of our ancestors,

Place of our family's birth.

In your graceful peace

We feel the surety

Of our presence.

In the streams and rivers

That define you

We hear the whisper

Of voices and souls of ourselves passed.

Those who watch and guide us still.

Nature isle, Dominica.

We are, and will always be

Yours.

Dominoes and Rum

The green baize board is laid down with reverence on the table.

Drinks are lined up ready for the waiting contestants

Dark hands, hardened by work in foundries factories and dark coal pits

Caress the white ivory of the 'bones'

Scattered on the dark cloth

Rattle and clicking as these small shapes

are turned and spun face down on the surface

Slam! With a crack like shattering glass the first hits the table

Slam! Slam! Slam!

In quick succession the shapes begin to form

as each domino takes its place

Elders playing, heads bowed and eyes darting

As silent messages are passed

from one partner to the next

The occasional sip of white rum or dark Brandy

Placed aside him by an unseen hand.

Burning the throat for a moment, the liquid slips down to rest inside, warming his soul and centre.

Serious talk.

Patois littering the air

Playing mind games.

Games, not of aggression but of wit and partnership.

Teeth flashing and heads thrown back,

laughing at the scent of victory, or the witness of loss.

A relief from stress… from life.

Once played for bread, fish or johnny cakes,

now played for drinks, for purpose, for position

but always with passion.

Talking of the old days and drinking rum.

Dominoes.

The sport of our kings

5 THE BATHROOM

"Spaces for self-care, cleansing and hearing silences – the only place for solitude in a noisy world."

THE BATHROOM: STORIES OF CLEANSING AND REFLECTION

The bathroom in my mother's house had two distinct phases. Two identities which reflect not only how it changed over time, but also how my association with it developed as I grew.

In the early years when we lived in my mother's house, the bathroom was the original one; common to many council houses in the 1970s. The minimum number and style of fittings were installed, a bath, a toilet, and a sink. The large white cast iron bath took up the whole of the wall to the left of the door. The toilet was positioned opposite the door, to the right of the widow at the 'tap end' of the bath with the sink between it and the bath. On your right as you entered the room, high above a child's reach, was an electric heater with a pull cord, which, an appropriate adult could turn on when the bathroom became too cold. My mother used to switch on the heater just before we got into the bath. This took the chill off a very cold room. Because you see, this was the 1970s, a time before central heating - there was no other way to heat the bathroom and the single glazed frosted glass, with its metal frame that bounded all the windows when we first moved into the house, provided little insulation from the weather outside.

My sisters and I bathed together in that bath. Myself as the eldest of the three, had to sit at the 'tap end', my next sister down sat at the opposite end, with our youngest sister in the middle. When we were very young, my mother supervised our bathing directly and made sure we were washed head to foot. As we grew older she directed us to not only wash ourselves - but also to sit in line one behind the other and wash the back of the sister in front of us switching sides at the end to make sure my back was washed too. Interestingly my youngest sister had her back washed twice in this arrangement – but that did not seem to matter.

The best part about the weekly bath was having time to play in what was left of the soap suds with a cup, a flannel and occasionally a small toy. Myself and my sisters talked incessantly, making shapes in the soapsuds from the bubbles. We drew pictures on each other's backs through the thick Imperial Leather soap that we'd smeared between our shoulder blades. The white soap against our gleaming dark skin creating a contrasting canvas for our 'art'. We played guessing games and drew our names on each other before the bubbles disappeared. A particular favourite of ours was a guessing game involving this riddle..

"I draw a snake upon your back half it, quarter it, DIP! which finger did that?"

We stayed in that water until our fingers began to wrinkle and the water turned cold. Occasionally our mother would agree to our begging for five more minutes and would carry up a kettle of boiling water to top up the bath. A quick step out of the bath while the water was poured and then we were back in with the additional heat allowing us to continue our games for a while longer. When time was up my mother held up the large towel and one by one, in age order, from youngest to eldest – we removed ourselves from the bath, were dried vigorously and moisturised head to toe. As we grew older and could not easily fit into the bath together, my youngest sister was removed, bathed separately and the other two of us were trusted to bath, wash our hair and completed the essential moisturising rituals ourselves.

In the 1970s, when we moved into my mother's house, central heating was not the only thing missing. We also did not have an automatic washing machine and as a consequence, the large white bath was used to cleanse clothes as well as bodies.

My sister and I helped my mum in this task. My mother prepared the washing early in the morning – first by liberally covering the clothes laying in the bath with washing powder from the big box that she kept in the kitchen pantry, then running the bath taps until they were covered – occasionally swishing the clothes around in a circle until just the right amount of 'suds' had been created. My sister and I watched carefully – after all – we knew that day would come when we had to take over this part of the preparations. Once my mother was happy with the water/suds/clothes mixture, we left the bathroom for a while to allow the clothes to 'soak'. This was just enough time for my mother to make a cup of tea for us all and for us to finish any incomplete or 'substandard' tidying up in our bedroom.

When our chores were complete (or my mother called us) my sister and I joined my mother and set about with the washing task in hand. We all knelt down next to each other besides the bath and washed, by hand, the clothes that were piled inside. When we first started, my sister and I were responsible for the smallest items while my mother took over for the sheets, towels and heavy jumpers. Each piece of washing was grasped tightly and rubbed between our clenched hands, dipping the item back into the water periodically to keep it wet and soapy. After every few rubs the clothes were squeezed hard – listening out for the 'cheep!' sound they made as the soap was forced through the fibres – my mother taught us to listen out for that sound as a sign we had sufficient soap on the garment. This continued until the suds coming out of the item ran white with no sign of dirt. The clothes then needed to be wrung out, the water released from the bath and fresh water added to the bath for rinsing, this was repeated until all the clothes were cleaned and the water ran clear. The weight of some of the clothes made them hard to lift and squeeze out the water so these items we did between us – starting at opposite ends - lifting and squeezing in unison until we met in the middle.

Washing clothes for a family of seven was a mammoth task and took a long time. The water often went cold before the chore was complete – once again, before we had central heating, my mother carried a kettle or pan of boiling water upstairs and added to the bath. Our knees sometimes became numb from kneeling on the lino that covered the bathroom floor and we had to stand, give them a rub, and occasionally even run on the spot until they felt better. Before retaking our kneeling position and continuing. Doing the laundry in this way was a glimpse of the work it took to run the house.

During these times my mother and us girls spoke of many things – we sang songs (mainly hymns), told each other jokes and asked questions of each other. Occasionally the radio played while we worked, and my mother would wow us by knowing the words to the latest pop sings as well as having critical opinions on the news items.

As we washed the clothes in that bathroom we learned about my mother's thoughts on the world, we learned the meaning of duty and hard work as part of what makes a family strong – getting things done together and sharing thoughts along the way. It's hard to believe when I look back now that not only did we do this task weekly, kneeling by the bath, but my mother did this herself for many years before my sister and I were old enough to help

A few years later, the bathroom underwent a transformation. This occurred after my parents had been able to buy the house alongside many other former council tenants as part of the national 'Right to buy' scheme in the late 1970s. The white cast iron bath was replaced with a shower cubicle and the white toilet and sink were exchanged for similar items in peach – proudly bearing the name 'Armitage Shanks'. And the bath? Well, the smallest bedroom in my mother's house – positioned next door – became the new bathroom. A matching peach bath, complete with 1980s matching bath shelving, plus a sink with attached peach bathroom cabinet now graced the space. The clear glass window was now frosted (and double glazed). We had become a two-bathroom family! Much more suited to a growing brood needing to get washed dressed and out of the house individually rather than washing in groups of boys and girls!

The new bathroom was almost exclusively used by my mother and us children. I have no memory of my dad ever using that bathroom – he liked the shower – it suited him with his early morning rising to get to work before 6am, his late night returns from playing dominoes and hanging out with his friends. A quick shower and a shave in the small mirror on the windowsill – and he was good. Slowly, the old bathroom – the new shower room, became dad's – with us only entering to use the toilet. His washbag and shaving stuff sat on the windowsill. The only signs of my mother's influence here was the plant on the windowsill.

The addition of the new bathroom, separate to the toilet brought with it a new era. One where the bathroom became a place of solitude – in a large family, the bathroom was one of the only places in my mother's house where you could be by yourself. Bathing became a time to think, relax, reflect and rewind. Alone with your thoughts – and fears. A time to dream of great things without the pressure of someone knocking on the door for you to 'make haste' because they needed to use the toilet.

The new bathroom in all its peach glory saw me through from childhood to adulthood. The place where I lingered before first getting my O level results, and later my A levels. The place where I witnessed the physical and emotional changes in myself and my family as we grew. The emotional rollercoaster of puberty and the shock realising that the 'period talk' given by my mother (during one of our washing sessions many moons ago) – was true! – Love, laughter, grief and loss; emotions often expressed silently in the quiet space of the bathroom. I processed them all, as I bathed or prepared myself for the day ahead in that bathroom, in my mother's house.

Washday 1

The large pink wash basket gave up its contents once more.

Her hands shifted and sorted the piles of fabric with precision into multiple types.

With a sigh and a quick twist of her wrists

she heaves the weight into the bath.

Water gushes from the taps onto the items

Their colours darkening as they thirstily drink the fluid.

Soap and water mix eagerly

Forming white peaks and valleys

amongst the clothes beneath.

We watch as her hands cut swathes through the water,

Swirling from left to right, and back again

Until she is satisfied.

A quick look from her

And we are ready.

Stepping forward,

Bending down,

The hard floor beneath our knees

and the hot water buried up to our elbows.

Dip

Wet

'Cheep!'

The rhythmic sounds of hands at work

Accompanied by our chatter, laughter and song.

She continues to hum without missing a beat.

Her hands moving twice as fast as ours

…dip….wet, cheep…

Until all signs of yesterday, and last week, are gone.

I Remember the Heater

I remember the heater

It's toothy grin standing over us

Awaiting its call to duty at my mother's command

The familiar 'click' of the chord springs it into life.

Its orange smile,

fills the room with heat and light.

I remember the heater

Standing guard over our games

And artistic attempts on a soapy canvas.

Silently keeping score as to the passage time

From its place above my mother's head.

I remember the heater

Against the whitewashed wall

Its former bright silver coat, now mottled and

tarnished

by the damp atmosphere and the passing of years.

its power beginning to fade.

Intermittent gaps appear

Like the toothless smile of an ageing parent.

I remember the heater.

A space left by its absence

As colourful tiled paper cover the screw holes

left by its departure.

Its work completed,

No longer essential.

No longer seen

But I remember the heater.

Wash Day 2

The water gleams

As I pour it down my sisters back.

Like silver the light reflects

Against the flawless warm chocolate

Of her skin.

The soap gives up its familiar fragrance

As I rub it in my hands.

She wriggles and laughs

As I try to wash her back

And do it right

Under my mother's watch full eyes.

My brow is furrowed

As I concentrate on the agreed task

'Drawing a perfect face'

On the soapy canvas in front of me.

Before I can finish, she has had enough

And spins to face me.

I turn, and focus on trying not to squirm

From her small tickly fingers

Working their own masterpiece.

My sister starts the familiar round

Singing loudly

I take up the refrain

"London's burning... London's burning"

Our young voices rising

With the steam and melting

Into the atmosphere.

My mother watches

Smiling and clapping at our efforts.

Hair washed; body clean

We step out into her embrace

Framed by the large towel which she wraps around us

Still singing. Always smiling.

Hello Stranger

The mirror watches as I stare back

The face is familiar

I first saw her as I stood on tip toes to see

The whole of her looking back at me

I watch as the roundness of youth

Which framed her mouth and jaw

Are replaced with a more streamlined form.

The smile remains the same

It's almost a grin.

Teeth white and even

Shining through her broad mouth

energetic and eager to please.

Never quite able to master the coyness

or reserved smile of others

Now occasionally framed with lipstick.

- Very occasionally.

Stepping back, the mirror acknowledges

Longer legs and slender arms

Which have formed almost unnoticed

From her one time unfeasibly slim limbs

That were once the source of teasing bye brothers

Or concern from those whose job it was

Two weigh and check our progress –

"So thin"- does she eat??

I hold her gaze and she holds mine

I'm nod in recognition

Of our changing form

The eyes remain the same

They haven't changed.

They never do.

I smile

And the familiar stranger, smiles back.

Private Spaces

A place to think

A place to breathe out

And to take time.

To allow the mind to be free

Free to wander and wonder

About all the things

Real and imagined

That make up the world.

A place to relax

To revive and refresh the mind

As much as the body.

A silent space in a world

Crammed with company.

A place legitimately yours

When all else must be shared.

A place to find space.

Space to imagine,

Rehearse and replay times past.

And times yet to come.

A place to be

To hope and to dream.

A space to allow

Feelings to escape, unfettered.

To fully express the emotions

Of our experiences.

To laugh, to cry,

to smile, to feel.

A space for privacy

A place of privacy

A place for all of us.

Personal Care

In the silent spaces of my mind
I hear the sounds often drowned out
By the noises of life.
As the warm waters cover me
I am held in an embrace
Which soothes and coaxes me to think,
To be aware of the whole of myself.
In this place, at this time.

The people, actions and impressions of the day
Are played out before me
Like an old cine film.
Some colours more vivid
In stories that make me smile,
Stop or catch my breath.
I am carried by the emotion
That follows each scene.

Living and reliving

The actual and imagined possibilities

Of the events.

Weightless and fearless

In the cradle of these waters

I am blessed with a boldness

And freedom

Surpassing any that exist

In my reality.

With each breath I feel myself relax

Exhaling the tensions, insecurities

And hesitations of the day

The stillness of the air

And the sounds of the gentle movements of water

Brings mindful clarity and peace.

As body and soul are cleansed, in unison.

Every part of me in tune with the other.

Once more whole.

Once more sure.

Once more

6 THE BEDROOM

Our space – Togetherness, connection and renewal.

THE BEDROOM: STORIES OF PERSONAL AND PRIVATE SPACES

There were 4 bedrooms in my mother's house.

The largest bedroom, at the top of the stairs and opposite the bathroom was my parents' bedroom. Next to that along the corridor, also facing to the front of the house was another large double bedroom I shared with my sisters. My brothers, when they still lived at home, had the room at the end of the corridor which looked out over the garden. The bedrooms were gender divided and remained so until my brothers left home.

The smallest bedroom, before it became the bathroom was never actually used as a bedroom. It also looked over the back garden but was previously used by my mother to store her sewing machine, fabrics, the ever full wash basket (bright pink and plastic as it was) and all the clothes for the laundry. In later years, this small room was changed into the peach bathroom and all the items listed – except the wash basket – moved into the back bedroom previously occupied by my brothers.

But let's get back to bedrooms.

My parents' bedroom like the front room was a no go area for children. On the few occasions we were allowed to go in, it always smelled of powder. Perfumed talcum powder – provided by Avon to be exact. The large bed with its oversized headboard and integrated bedside tables took up most of the room. An electronic radio alarm clock watched the room from one of the bedside tables. The side where my dad slept. This was balanced by an ornament and a bottle of Holy water in the shape of the Virgin Mary on my mother side. Each, however standing on an equally well crocheted doily.

I never quite knew what was in the small drawers at my dad's side of my parents' bed, because I never really went in it. I was never asked to.

I know my mother kept her medication in the drawer on her side as often in the early mornings when we bought her a cup of tea, we would open the drawer, hand them to her, and she laid them out on the bedside table. On other occasions she could be seen sitting on the edge of the bed, drawer open, checking her tablets.

My parents' bedroom had two windows. Both looking over the front of the house. Between the two windows was a large teak dressing table. Which groaned under the strain of the many bottles of lotions, potions, creams and oils that adorned it. Almost all of which, had been purchased at different times from the Avon Lady. My mother loved Avon. Powder puffs with huge circular containers of loose powder fought for space with ornaments, religious symbols, and my mother's many Jewelry boxes. These boxes of various sizes and colours spilled over with chains, rings, broaches and earrings. Few of which I actually saw her wear, but which were always there.

As younger children, when we were very lucky, we were allowed to sit on her bed as she went about her chores, look through, sort the earrings and play with them. At the bottom of the bed was a small double wardrobe which held my father's clothes. To the left of the bed was a large wardrobe with a large mirror triple in size indeed it took up the full wall, this held my mother's clothes.

My parent's bedroom was a place where we never went unless invited. Invited or not, the knock before you entered my parents' bedroom was essential. Woe betides you if you entered without knocking first.

As a young child, I do remember sometimes waking up very early before my sisters, after my father had gone to work and knocking on my parents' bedroom door. My quiet knock would be met by my mother saying "Laura?" which was my pass to enter. Silently my mother would turn and lift the bedcovers so I could crawl into her bed and sleep against her warm back until it was time to get up for school.

The girls bedroom next door (our bedroom),was almost as large as my parent's bedroom. It held a large double bed and when we were younger, the three of us slept in that bed. Myself as the eldest on the outside, my second sister next to the wall, and my younger sister in the middle. As we grew older and space became a premium, my parents inserted a single bed into the bedroom. On which I slept while my two sisters, continued to sleep in the double bed.

Double beds were a feature in our house. My brothers' bedroom also had a double bed. Part of the reasoning for this was that when any relatives or guests stayed, particularly adults, then we were decanted out of the double bed – to sleep either on the floor or double up with each other. In one of the other rooms, sometimes even sleeping end to end like sardines to make space. And of course, at the regular parties, we slept end to end, or crammed together with our cousins and friends as the party rumbled on downstairs.

My sisters and I shared the bedroom up until I left the house at the age of 18.

When my brothers left, we occasionally also slept or had access to the bedroom at the back. But the best times I remember as a young child and through my time in my mother house is lying in the dark, talking with my sisters, laughing and giggling and playing games. Singing the repertoire of songs we had learned: Whether they were hymns, pop songs, or ditties we made up for ourselves. I never needed much sleep, even as a young child and one my earliest memories is lying awake and it being dark. That's probably why I was never afraid of the dark.

We were always sent to bed at the same time. That was the rule.

Often long after we stopped talking and my sisters were asleep, I was still awake. I often listened to my sister's gentle breathing and the occasional snore, as they slept. Occasionally I would sneak downstairs slowly and quietly and walked back into the living room where my parents were watching the TV. Sometimes my mother would rise, make me a hot chocolate and allow me to sit with them for an hour while I drank it and then say to me "it's time to go back to bed", walking me soundlessly back to our room and into bed. Occasionally, though, with a 'look' and equally quickly I could be sent back to bed. I never knew which one was going to happen, but it was always worth the risk for the chance of the hot chocolate and a short time sitting between my parents in the flickering light of the TV.

When I had the single bed, which was laid against the wall between our bedroom and my parents' bedroom, I could often hear my parents talking quietly into the night. Discussing their days, discussing finance, discussing their children, and discussing our progress and our aspirations. I often fell asleep with the sound of their voices drifting in my ears.

I also listened from that bedroom to the sounds of my father waking very early in the morning. Him going into the bathroom and getting ready for work then descending the stairs quietly. Sometimes when my father woke early, I also went downstairs with him at 4:30 and sat in the kitchen at the kitchen table while he got ready for work. When he left at 5:00 o'clock, he asked me to go back upstairs and on those occasions, I knocked on the door of my mother's bedroom and sometimes was allowed to go and sleep with her until it was time to go to school.

The bedrooms in my mother house were private spaces, but they were also spaces for us children to have time together as siblings: To read and to discuss and to talk as we often did, long into the night. Here we watched the light fade behind the curtains and the sun rise again the next day. We told stories from the past and stories from the present. Things that happened to us. Things we found funny and things that made us laugh uncontrollably. We whispered, secrets between us.... And gave good advice.

Or so we thought.

In the early morning, before it was time to go downstairs, we'd sit on the floor, read our books, or play our games until it was time to get ready.

When we were sick in that bedroom, the person who was ill slept in the single bed with the other two watching from the distance from the double bed on the other side. The bedroom was another children's space, but different to the living room. It was a space for quiet, a space for coming together.

A space for *us* to set the rules.

Here we renewed our minds and our souls as much as our bodies. Refresh, Renew, recount and recall were symbols of the bedrooms in my mother's house.

What I remember most about the bedroom in my mother's house was the relative silence. In the small hours before my father awoke, the house was still. Its stillness only punctuated by the striking of the front room clock in the room below – on the hour and half hour- marking the passage of time when there was no other visible record. As I grew older, I welcomed those silent times as space to listen less to the house and its familiar sounds, but more to myself. I played and replayed my options, thoughts and feelings about life and my place within in. I reflected on the differences of opinion and action between myself, my sisters or my few close friends with whom I had shared my concerns. I agonised in turn about my choices, mistakes and hesitations but most importantly, I listened to how I truly felt and forgave myself.

In that bedroom, in the darkness of an almost silent room, I allowed myself to be human.

Old day

Watching the dimming light

As it slices through the darkness

From the chink

Where the curtains don't quite meet.

The streetlight blinks occasionally

As if to remind us of its presence.

Constantly watching over us and our neighbours.

The occasional sound of a car

Coming up the road

And passing the house.

Knowing it wasn't dad's car

- His has a particular sound.

As did his car door, as he slammed it shut.

The creak of our metal gate opening

followed by his measured steps

Coming up the path to our front door.

His key turning in the lock

Was always punctuated with the

Sound of my mother's cough through the wall

And the 'click' of her bedside lamp being switched off.

Signaling that her watch tonight is over.

We were all safely home.

The deep slow chime of the clock downstairs

Marks the passing of another hour.

Adult voices whispering in the night

lull me back to sleep as I turn my back to the wall

and close my eyes.

New Day

The buzz of dad's alarm clock wakes me again.

I listen as the movements of last night are reversed.

The low whispered voices through the wall

Speak of the day to come.

My mother laughs.

The sound of my dad rising and leaving their room fills my ears.

I listen as he stretches himself for the workday ahead.

Letting out that involuntary sigh, followed by a sharp inhalation.

The sound of the shower.

Him descending the stairs quickly, returning a few minutes later with what I know to be tea for my mother.

I slip from the bed and greet him at their bedroom door as he exits.

I smile.

He slowly shakes his head – but smiles all the same.

We descend the stairs together.

Without speaking he pours me some tea from his thermos

Into a small orange cup.

I sip it silently and watch him from the table.

He checks his workbag…and mouths soundlessly to himself: '*Snap, flask, towel and change to get a paper*'

He dons his jacket.

With a nod to me, he gestures upstairs.

No words yet spoken.

I follow him to the front door.

He stands waiting,

Watching as I quickly mount the stairs.

I turn and wave as I reach the top.

He nods.

Then opens and closes the door quietly.

As his steps fade, I return to bed.

The slam of the car door and the sound of his engine fills my ears.

I listen until I can no longer hear him.

And the daylight replaces the streetlight

In keeping watch.

It's Time

It's time to be still.

Time to relax, revive and recover.

Time to allow yourself to just, be.

Time to steady your breathing.

Time to remember and recall all that is good about yourself.

Time to release and let go of all that restricts your freedom.

And keeps you small.

Time to allow your thoughts to fly.

Time to reconnect with what makes you, uniquely you.

Time to give thanks.

Time to recognise the value and beauty of your life.

It's time to dream.

Knock Before Entering

Knock before entering the cave of wonders.

Where bright and sparling treasures are housed.

Knock before entering the place where problems are solved

And the secrets of life are told.

Knock before entering that holy place

where prayers are said,

and pleas sent up to a greater force

For us, for the family and the world.

Knock before entering that healing place.

Where sick bodies are cured, and troubled minds are calmed

By the power of loving care and 'bush tea'.

Knock before entering this resting place.

Where bodies tired from the heat of the furnace

And the pace of the hospital kitchens

Are finally able to find release.

Before the start of another day.

Knock before entering this private space.

Where adults dream of home

And hope for our futures.

Knock before entering.

Always knock first.

Night Whispers

"Are you awake?"

The small voice whispers into the darkness.

"yes"

Comes the reply.

Warm bodies stretch and legs reach for the places where the sheets still hold onto their coldness.

"Are you ok?"

The question hangs for a moment

Then is met with the reply

"I'm ok but I can't sleep – tell me a story"

I talk to you of lovely things, of butterflies and bees and places where mermaids swim.

Hands reach out and clasp each other.

Stories begin and songs are sung.

Voices combining, releasing melodies and

drawing pictures from our tales into the darkness.

On the waves of our tales, hearts and, minds are soothed and breathing calms.

"Are you awake?"

The voice asks.

No, not anymore

The silence whispers back.

When I Heard My Own Silence

When I heard my own silence

…. I stopped saying 'Yes' when I really meant 'No'.

When I heard my own silence

…. I forgave myself for staying.

When I heard my own silence

…. I remembered I was good enough, just as I am.

When I heard my own silence

…. I realised that the ache in my stomach was my protection, not my weakness.

When I heard my own silence

…. I celebrated my difference.

When I heard my own silence

…. I refused to be someone else's action point.

When I heard my own silence

…. I realised speaking up was a choice, my choice.

When I heard my own silence

…. I saw the power I had and the responsibilities it held.

When I heard my own silence

.... Slowed my breathing, and relaxed.

When I heard my own silence

.... I allowed myself to be human; perfectly
imperfect, me.

7 THE HALLWAY

Passages in time – Hellos and Goodbyes – Flights between what was, what is and what will be.

THE HALLWAY: STORIES OF BECOMING

The hallway was the final room in my mother's house.

You may wonder or question. Whether a hallway is a room at all. And if so. Why is it the last room?

Well, we will get to that.

The hallway was a standard length for a former Council house. At one end. Was the aluminium framed double glazed front door and at the other, the door to the kitchen.

Standing at the front door, looking in, the stairs rose up to the right of you. You could glimpse the toilet and later shower room door at the top. The door to the front room, which was also glazed, was on your left. The only other door in the space was that to the under stairs coats cupboard. This housed the electric metre, outdoor coats, an array of shoes and the Hoover. I remember soon after we moved in my dad and uncle spending a Saturday afternoon making the door from hardboard - Which transformed the space under the stairs into that cupboard.

The hallway was light and airy, helped by the window to the right at the bottom of the stairs as well as the glazed doors on all sides.

Like many Caribbean houses of the time, the carpet that dressed the hallway and stairs. Was a brightly coloured patterned affair. At the time, almost psychedelic. It was the most expensive floor covering in my mother's house. And to protect it, yet still allow its beauty to show, my father had laid a clear plastic runner from the front door to the kitchen to guide your way.

Above the door to the kitchen, directly opposite the front door, at the end of the plastic runway was a framed inscribed 'picture'. I have seen the same picture many times in the houses, of relatives and friends from the Caribbean:

"Christ is the head of this house.

The unseen guest at every meal.

The silent listener to every conversation"

Children and adults alike were left in no doubt as to what was expected of them as they passed under that sign.

Or who was watching -When my mother wasn't.

All in all, the hallway was an advert of my mother's love of colour and signalling our respectability to all who entered.

The walls of the hallway were white. Easy to clean and touch up as necessary. Essential in a house with so many children. On the wall, at the facing the bottom of the stairs, immediately to the right of the front door, was a gold metal framed mirror which tracked your ascent and descent in the house. It also acted as a last chance for my mother to check her church hat or dad to straighten his tie before leaving the house.

Below the mirror on a small table, sat the telephone, a large green Bakelite affair with a dial at the front. The kind everybody had in the 1970s and 80s, but which in modern times are an expensive collector's items. The phone was never locked. As I had seen it done in my friends' mothers' houses. It did not need to be locked. As it would never have occurred to us to use it without permission. Who, who would we be ringing anyway? Our friends equally didn't have access to the phone in their parents' houses.

I remember one occasion when one of my teenage brothers attempted to secretly lift the receiver and even before the tell-tale 'Ping' from the phone, my mother's voice had risen from the kitchen, demanding "Who's on the phone?'

It was years later. When I had left home and I was visiting, that I discovered that from its position at the bottom of the stairs, the mirror allowed you to see what was happening on the stairs or upstairs from my mother's usual vantage point of the table, sink or cooker in the kitchen……

The hallway, like all the rooms in my mother's house. Had a purpose, a place in our lives. It was more than the threshold into the house itself. It was the room for comings and goings.

The antithesis to the kitchen. The hallway was the entrance to the house for the important guests and visitors. The entry portal for adults.

Information from the outside came via the hallway.

By mail, parcel deliveries and news. Transitions and changes in the family and affecting the family came through here too. Received, translated, and shared by my parents. News of my grandmother's death. Births, sickness, triumphs and challenges. We first met them all in this space.

The transitions included us too.

As children we only entered or left the House via the front door If we were accompanied by an adult. Only when we reached later teenage years, were we given a front door key - and allowed to let ourselves in and out via the hallway.

It was via the hallway that we learned of our exam results. I remember sitting on the stairs in 1980, watching the brown envelope which held my 'O'level results as it rested under plastic runner at the front door. I sat and watched it for hours, it seemed. Until my mother descended the stairs, picked it up, and read them out to me. My success at that point. Signalled that I'd be able to enter the sixth form to do 'A' levels. And subsequently, 2 years later, I would be going to study for my degree.

It was via that hallway that my brothers left home - and returned with partners and later children of their own.

The opening and closing of the front door witnessed our changes as a family. From seven members to four, by the time I left home at 18 to start my nurse training at Sheffield City Polytechnic.

So, the hallway was indeed a room.

A room with a purpose: Signalling our individual transitions from child to adult - And our collective change as a family.

A threshold to life outside my mother's house.

Decades later, it was via the hallway that my mother passed peacefully to leave the house for the last time.

A transition of a different, more permanent kind.

The hallway.

Truly the final room in my mother's house.

Crossing the Threshold

The ebbing and flowing movements of the day.

Comings and goings signified by

the opening and closing of the portal.

Entry into the light and airy spaces

Of this place.

A place to rest

And put down burdens

Carried through the hours of exile.

Removing the coverings

Which sheltered us

From the storms and cold outside.

No longer needed in this safe space.

Permission to exhale,

To put down your guard

And open up to the warm comforting welcome

That awaits behind her smile.

Time to exhale, and also allow

The love to enfold you

And cradle you in its protective hold.

The access to the outside closes behind you.

Signalling your acceptance

And sanctuary.

The Key

Small.

Yet signifying

Something bigger than self.

Marking the passage

From child to adult

And all that life promises.

An indication of the trust

Now placed upon the holder.

The sure belief

That you are now able

To join others

And be the keeper of the gate.

Turning it over in your palm

It catches the light

And just for a moment

Sharp lines of light

Are sent into your mind's eye.

Delivering the clear message

Encased within it.

It is time.

Time to be grown.

Transitioning Well

Transitioning.

Moving from one life stage to the next.

Part of our human condition.

Mapping years passed

Through physical growth

And bodily changes.

Mirrored through the shifting shapes

and colours of the mind.

Born of experience,

Laughter and disappointments.

Each a lesson

Teaching us something of who we are.

What it means to be 'me'

In this world.

Transitioning.

Changing and being changed

By our time here on earth.

Shaping our minds and souls

Silently and seamlessly though actions.

A mixture of the purposeful

And the 'happenstance'

Those chance experiences

And hurried choices

That we had little time

To consider or to interrogate.

Transitioning well.

Allowing the self to be human.

In all our wonderful contradictions,

Craziness and calculations.

A deliberate decision

Choosing to see the light within us

When darkness is around.

A choice to feel the full impact

Of people, past and present,

Who have shaped our lives

And the paths we have taken

That have led us to he here

Right here,

Right now.

Leaving us uniquely equipped

To go forward,

To grow,

To fly.

Rites of Passage

From long gangly legs and incessant chatter.

Sliding downstairs

On our carpeted slopes.

Laughing, head back and teeth flashing.

As stairs are climbed, and descended

With equal speed – gifted by youth.

Racing siblings, cousins

And time.

To reach the unseen destinations

Disguised by time and space.

Sliding in stockinged feet

Across the plastic runway

Which spans the hidden worlds

Of the familiarity of home

And outside spaces.

Towards responsibility

And the joys of adventures

Yet unlived.

Crossing with increasing confidence

Between the two worlds

Of there, and here.

Simultaneously forming

And being formed

In mind and body.

Becoming a carrier of news

From worlds beyond.

Stories of people, places

And customs.

As different and varied from our own

As could be imagined.

Yet surprisingly, also familiar.

Physical, social and emotional changes

Marked by the passage of time

And the reflections in the glass.

Access to all rooms

And all conversations.

Indications of change, of trust

And of becoming.

Becoming grown.

Connections

Our stories are held in this space

This place between the rooms in our lives.

Stories of self

Which unite our past, present

And future selves.

Moving noiselessly through time

Marking the changes,

the comings and goings

of our time here.

This passage

Marking the crossing point

Of others

Entering and exiting our world.

Telling of us

And those who met us here.

Where we reside

Those who shaped our world

With their own gifts

Of presence and time.

Passing through

On their way

To a place in our hearts

Our minds, and our history.

Some staying for a moment

Their part played briefly – but importantly

At a particular point in time.

Others, becoming so entwined

In our lives,

Making it impossible to feel a time

when they were not known.

So central to who we are

as to become one of us.

Bless this House

Bless this house

And all who call, invited or otherwise

To rest, to shelter and to linger a while

Under her welcoming smile.

Reflecting the heart and soul

Of the queen and king who here reside.

Bless the hands that create the spaces

In which family, history and belonging

Are recorded, retold and relived

Allowing children and friends

To experience them, to know them

As if meeting in this life.

Bless the time we share

Living, laughing and growing together

With all the belief in our power and agency

Instilled over many years

And through unseen tears.

Building within and between us

Roots strong enough to withstand any cold.

Bless the dreams we have

Visions of becoming and belonging

Whispered in hallways

And shared in the dark.

Born on wings of hope and belief

Which carry us far beyond

This time and place.

8 SPEAKING FOR OURSELVES

We all have a voice and stories to tell.

But if we don't use that voice and speak for ourselves, others will speak for us. And at best, they may miss-tell our stories – and at worst, they will render us silent.

Professor Laura Serrant OBE

#SilenceSpeaks

ACKNOWLEDEGMENTS

This book was a long time coming.
It would not have been published without the support and encouragement of family and friends.

I want to thank my husband Mark without whose love and support I may never have found the peace in heart and mind to start writing this.

To my children Robert, Jack and Helena whose telling and retelling of their own stories of childhood inspired me to write some of mine.

A Special thanks to my talented daughter Helena for drawing the pictures and front cover.

To my siblings Tyson, Gilson, Lorelle and Maureen who lived with me in 'Our' Mother's house and are embedded in these pages as much as I am.

ABOUT THE AUTHOR

Professor Laura Serrant OBE is a global, multi-award-winning Leadership development and Inclusive practice specialist, professional speaker, and experienced coach. She is Director of her own consultancy Laura Serrant Limited.

Author of over 100 articles, including edited books and research, she is one of the BBC Expert women and was identified by The Health Service Journal among the top 50 leaders in three separate categories: Inspirational Women in Healthcare, BME Pioneers and Clinical Leader awards. She was named as the 8th most influential Black person in Britain by the Powerlist 2018. In 2018 she was awarded an OBE for services to Nursing and Health Policy.

She has a successful podcast series "Speaking for Ourselves" available across most social media platforms.

Her family are from The Commonwealth of Dominica, West Indies.

You can connect with Laura via:

Website: www.lauraserrant.com
Twitter: @lauraserrant
Instagram: lauraserrant2019
Linkedin: www.linkedin.com/in/prof-laura-serrant-obe

Printed in Great Britain
by Amazon

13490867R00098